SKOKIE PUBLIC LIBRARY

3 1232 01011 8794

D1129870

DISCOVER
DG
GRAPHICS

RAPUNZEL

BY JENNIFER FANDEL

ILLUSTRATED BY ANUKI LÓPEZ

PICTURE WINDOW BOOKS
a capstone imprint

Discover Graphics is published by Picture Window Books,
an imprint of Capstone.
1710 Roe Crest Drive
North Mankato, Minnesota 56003
www.capstonepub.com

Copyright © 2021 by Capstone. All rights reserved. No part of this
publication may be reproduced in whole or in part, or stored in a
retrieval system, or transmitted in any form or by any means, electronic,
mechanical, photocopying, recording, or otherwise, without written
permission of the publisher.

Library of Congress Cataloging-in-Publication Data is available on the Library of
Congress website.
ISBN: 978-1-5158-7118-7 (library binding)
ISBN: 978-1-5158-7274-0 (paperback)
ISBN: 978-1-5158-7125-5 (ebook PDF)

Summary: Revisit the tale of Rapunzel. The princess in the tower longs
for friends—and she finds one, in the shape of a curious prince. Will the
princess get her happily ever after, or grow old at the top of the tower?

Editorial Credits
Editor: Mari Bolte; Designer: Kay Fraser; Media Researcher:
Tracy Cummins; Production Specialist: Katy LaVigne

Printed in the United States
PA117

WORDS TO KNOW

cure—to make someone better

lonely—to feel sad from missing other people

promise—to say that you will do something in
the future

protect—to keep safe

rapunzel—a wild lettucelike herb that people
once gathered

CAST OF CHARACTERS

A **husband** and **wife** live together in the woods. The wife is pregnant and craves the herb rapunzel.

A **witch** lives next door. She has always wanted a child for herself.

Rapunzel grows up alone in a tower.

The **prince** is looking for a princess.

HOW TO READ A GRAPHIC NOVEL

Graphic novels are easy to read. Boxes called panels show you how to follow the story. Look at the panels from left to right and top to bottom.

Read the word boxes and word balloons from left to right as well. Don't forget the sound and action words in the pictures.

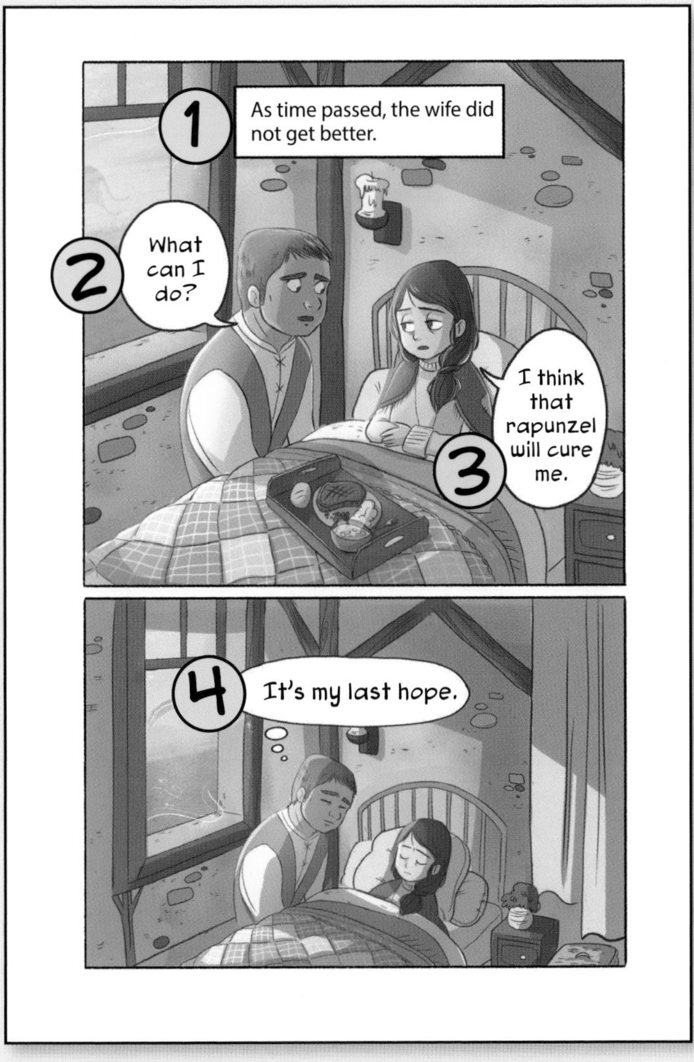
1 As time passed, the wife did not get better.
2 What can I do?
3 I think that rapunzel will cure me.
4 It's my last hope.

The pictures and the words work together to tell the whole story.

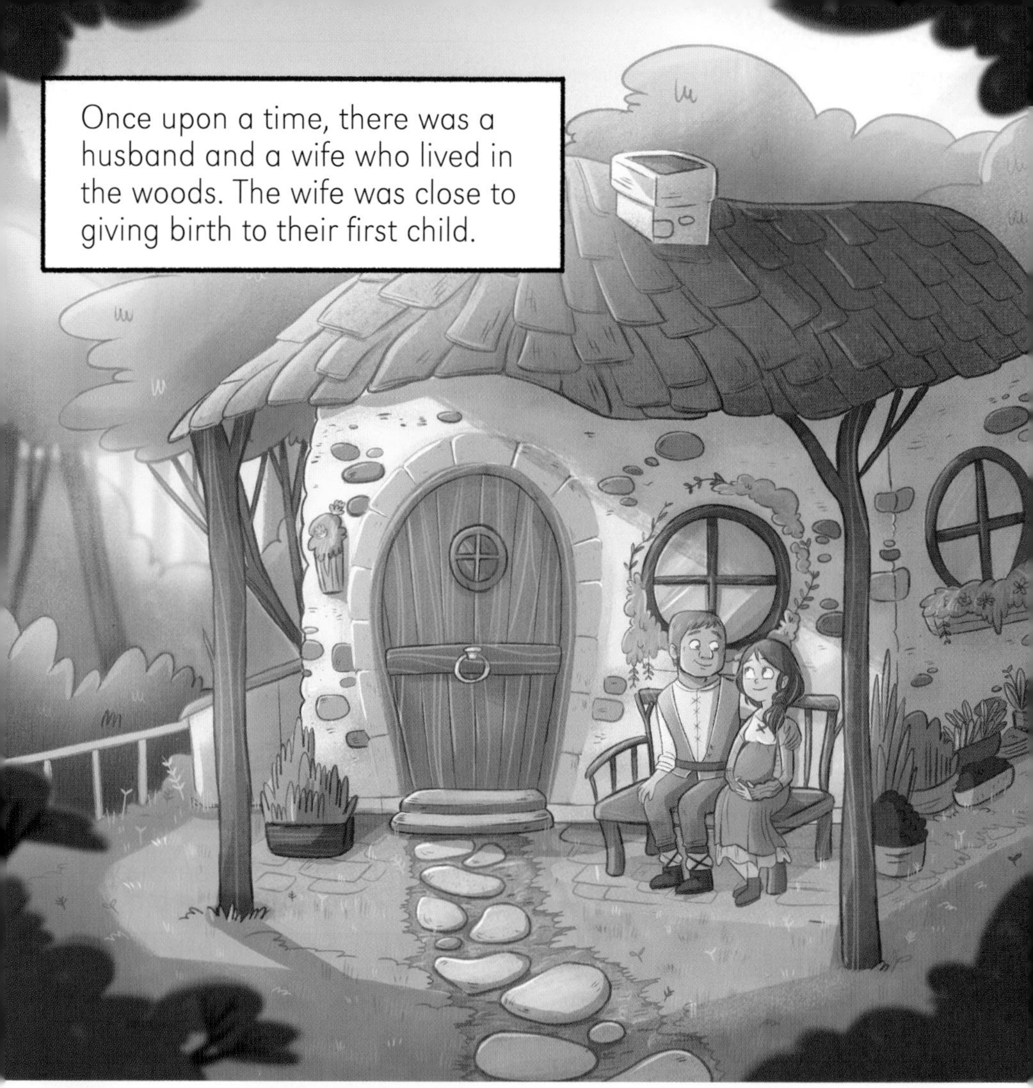
Once upon a time, there was a husband and a wife who lived in the woods. The wife was close to giving birth to their first child.

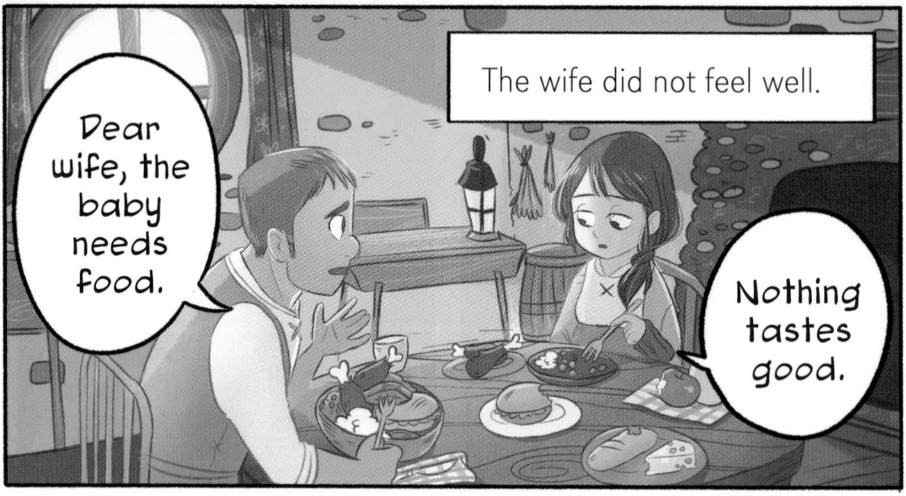
The wife did not feel well.
Dear wife, the baby needs food.
Nothing tastes good.

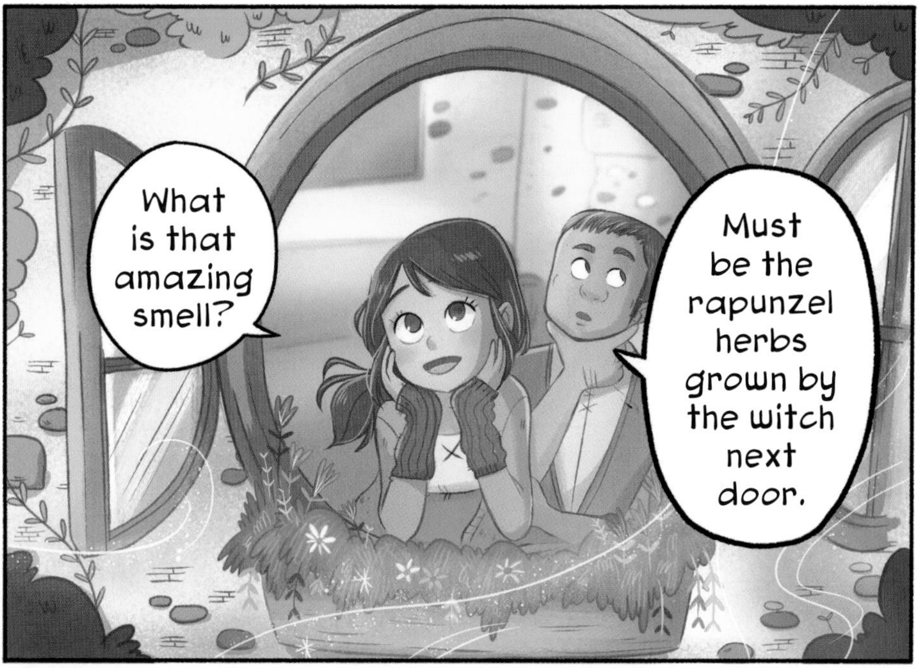
What is that amazing smell?
Must be the rapunzel herbs grown by the witch next door.

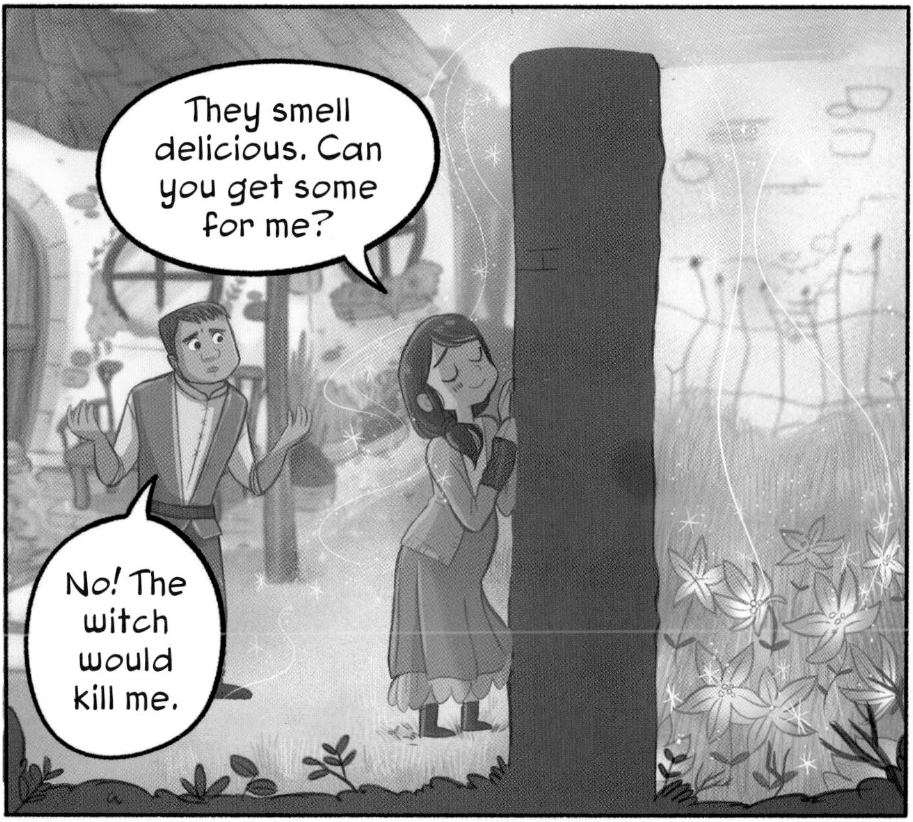
They smell delicious. Can you get some for me?
No! The witch would kill me.

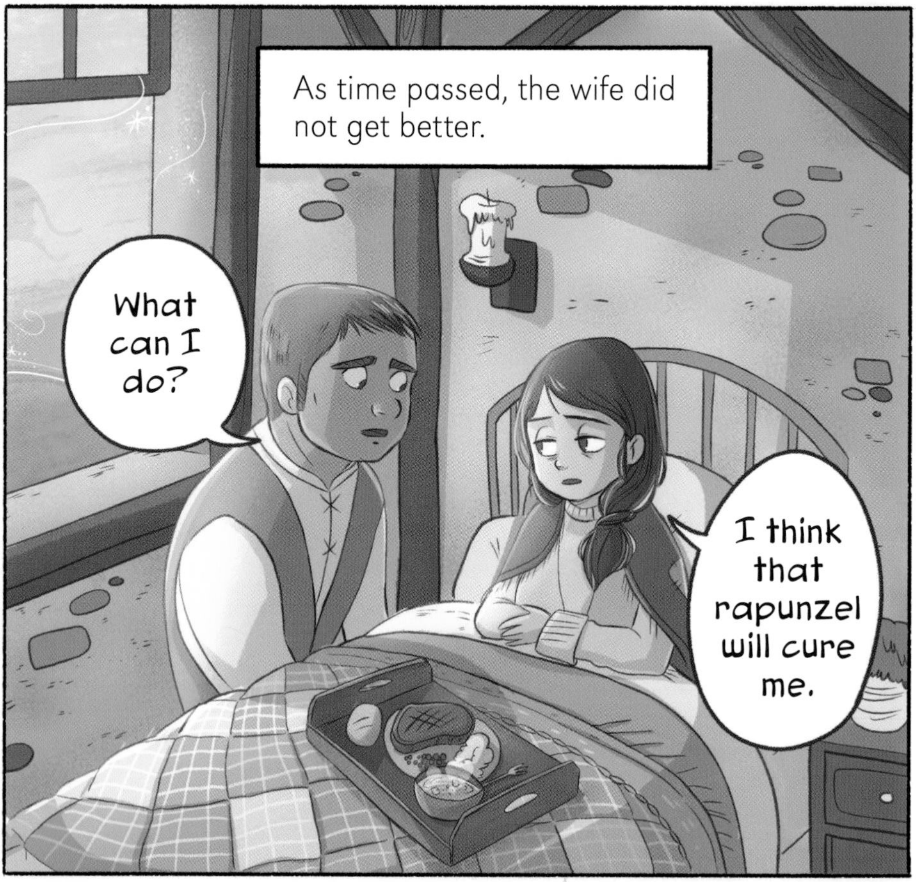
As time passed, the wife did not get better.
What can I do?
I think that rapunzel will cure me.

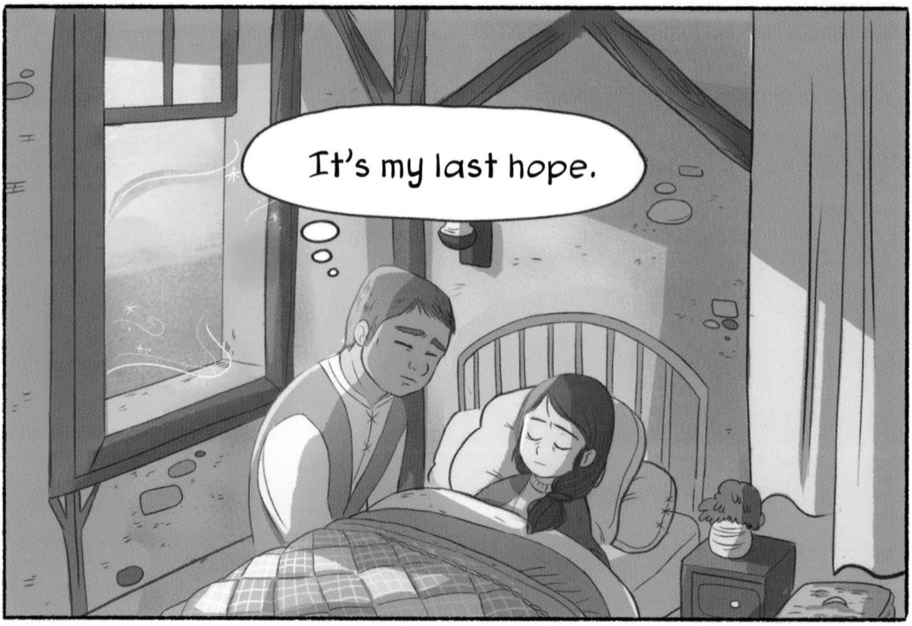
It's my last hope.

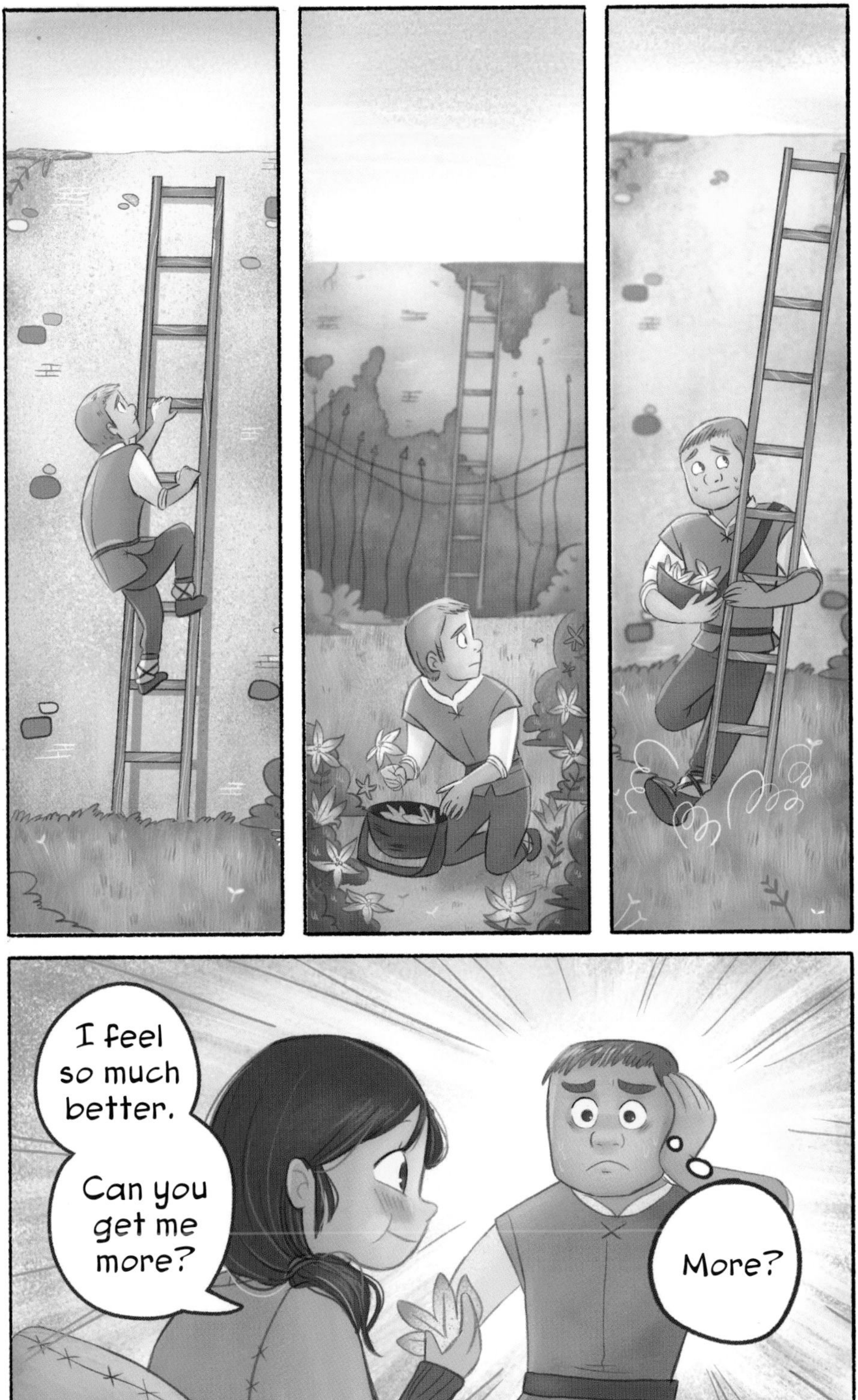
I feel so much better.
Can you get me more?
More?

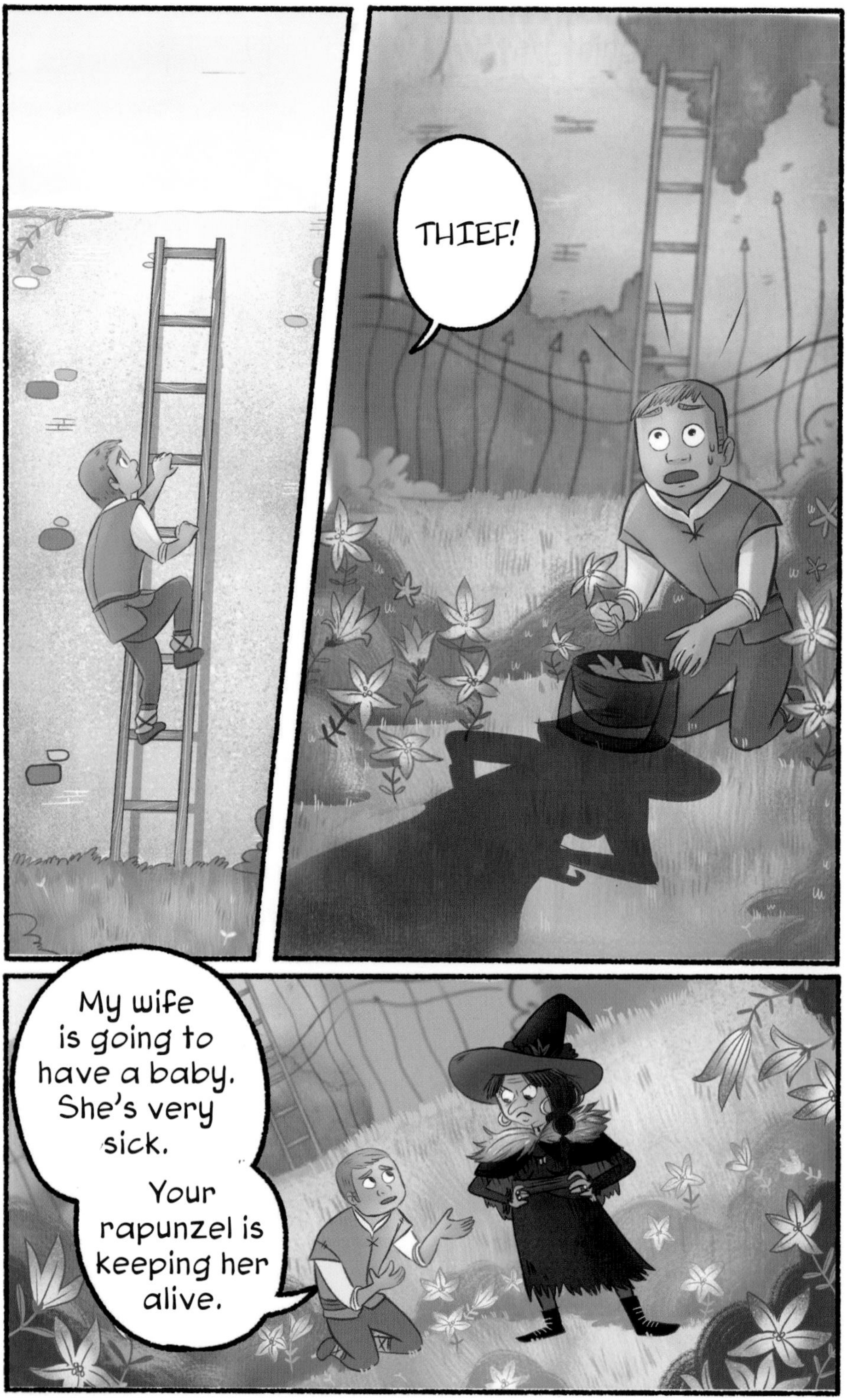
THIEF!
My wife is going to have a baby. She's very sick.
Your rapunzel is keeping her alive.

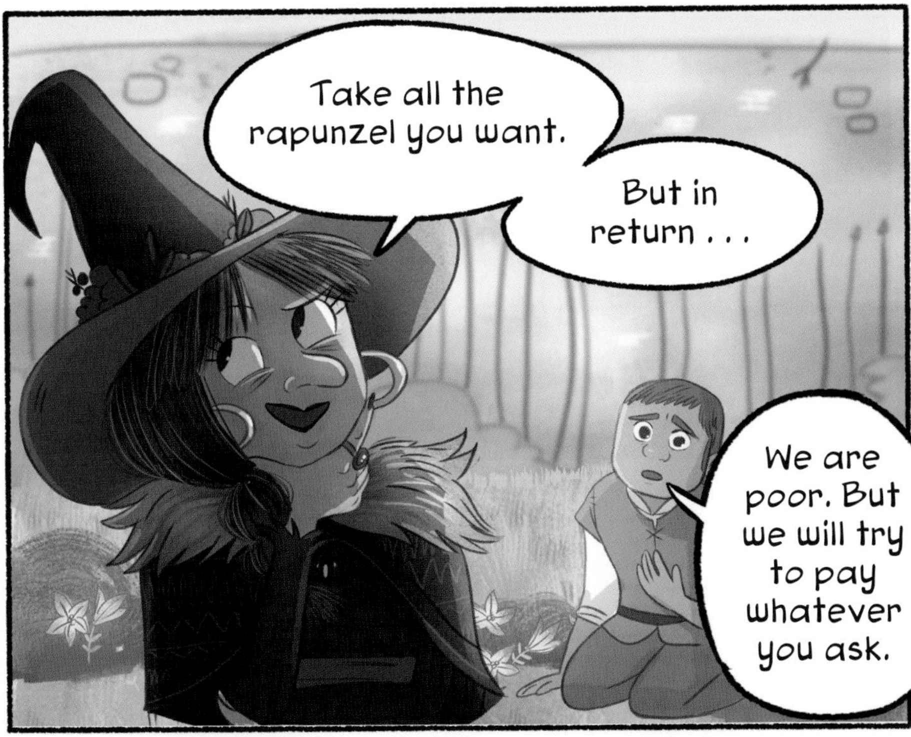
Take all the rapunzel you want.
But in return . . .
We are poor. But we will try to pay whatever you ask.

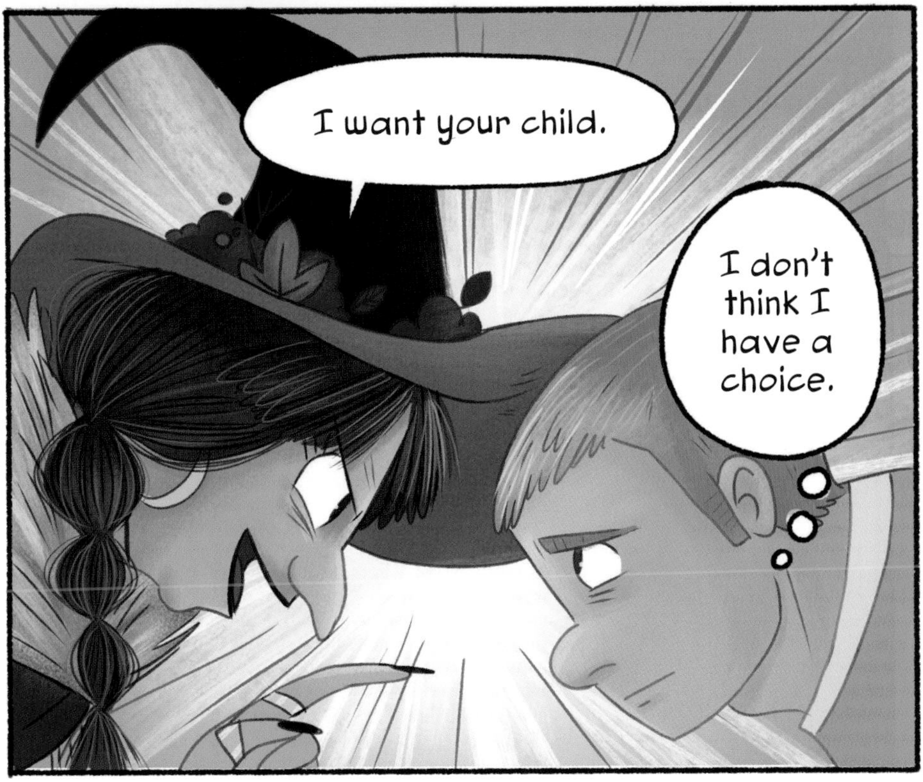
I want your child.
I don't think I have a choice.

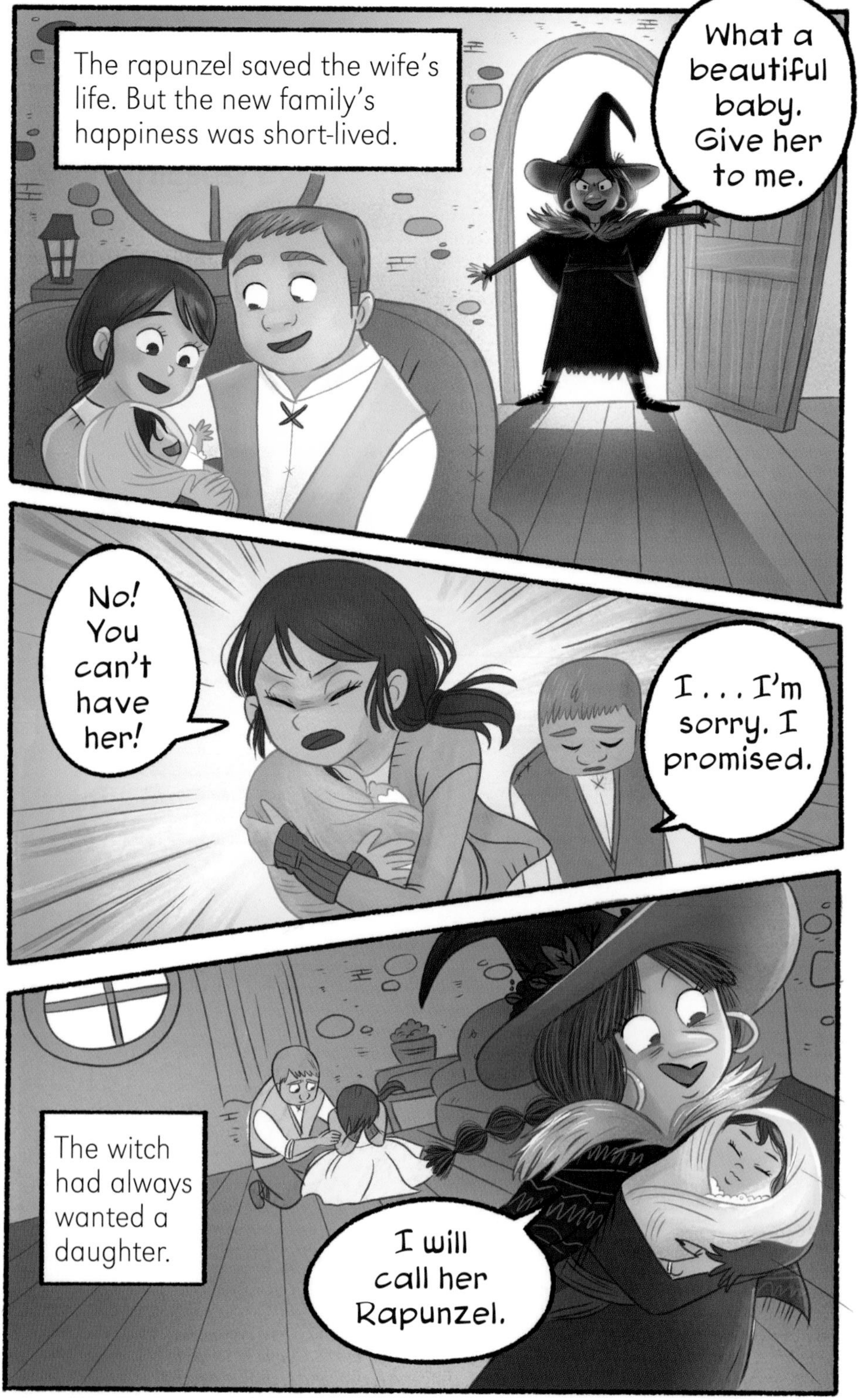

The rapunzel saved the wife's life. But the new family's happiness was short-lived.
What a beautiful baby. Give her to me.
No! You can't have her!
I . . . I'm sorry. I promised.
The witch had always wanted a daughter.
I will call her Rapunzel.

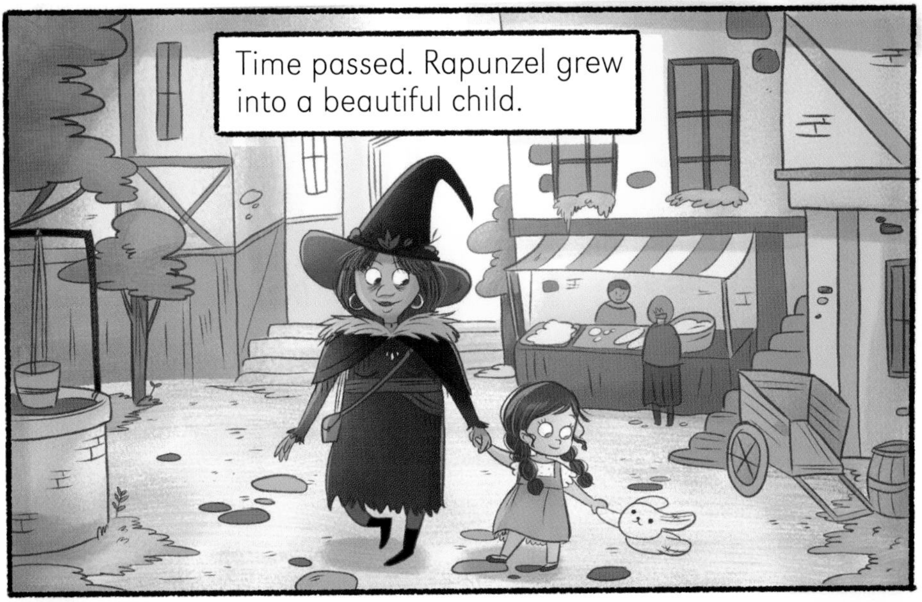
Time passed. Rapunzel grew into a beautiful child.

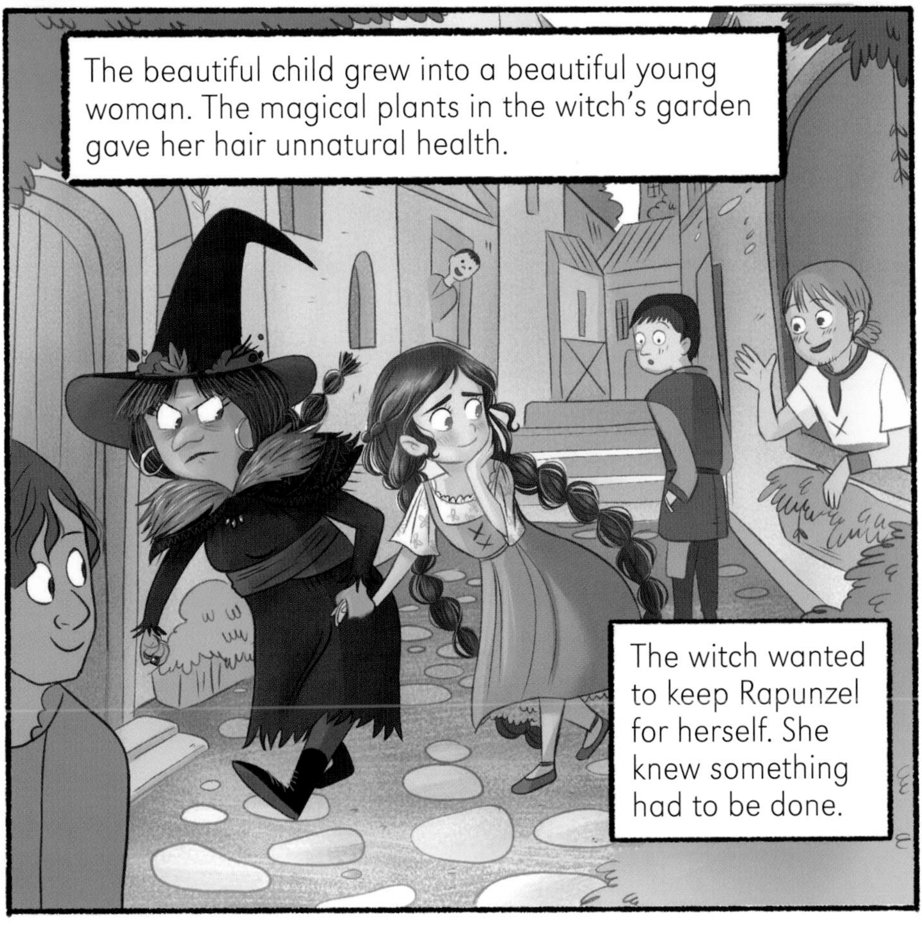
The beautiful child grew into a beautiful young woman. The magical plants in the witch's garden gave her hair unnatural health.
The witch wanted to keep Rapunzel for herself. She knew something had to be done.

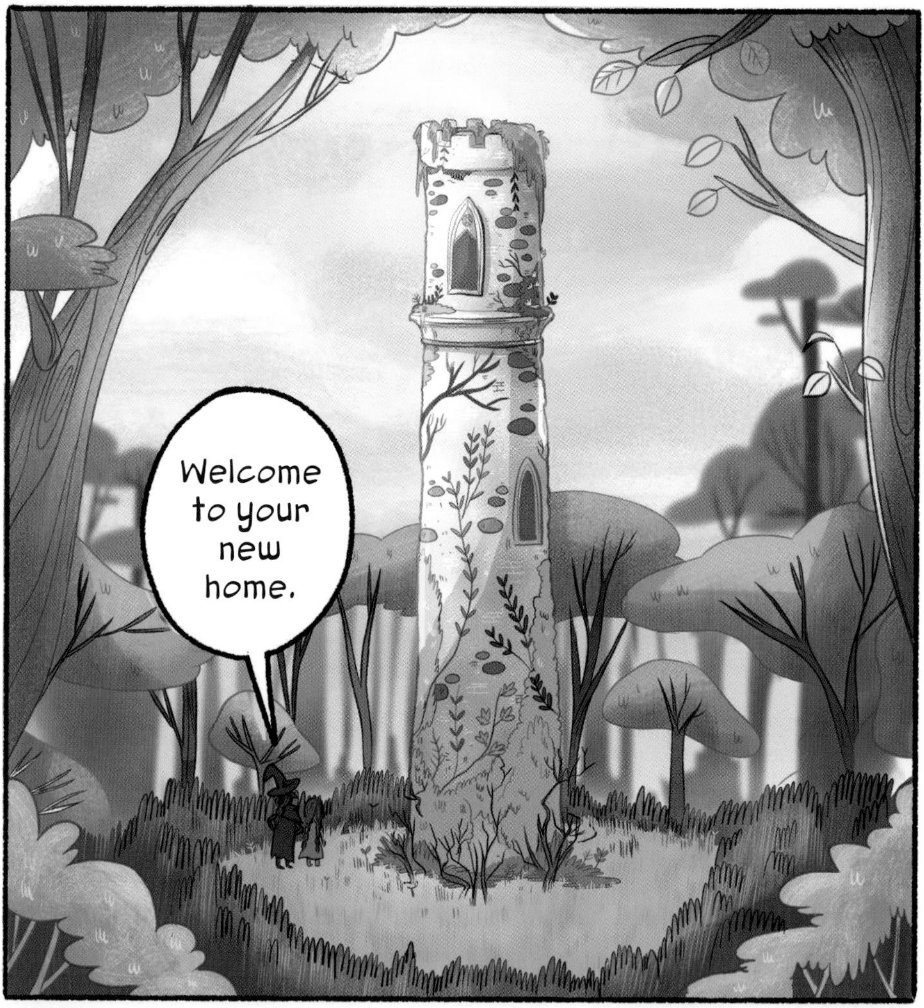
Welcome to your new home.

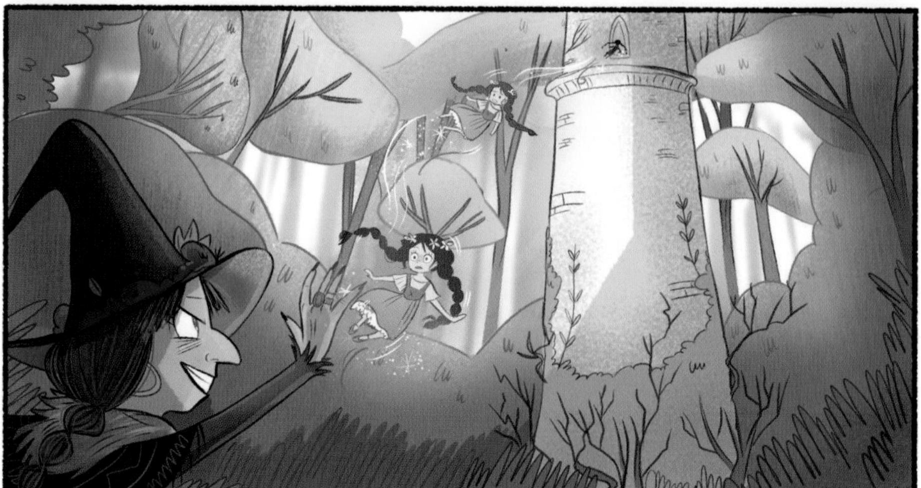

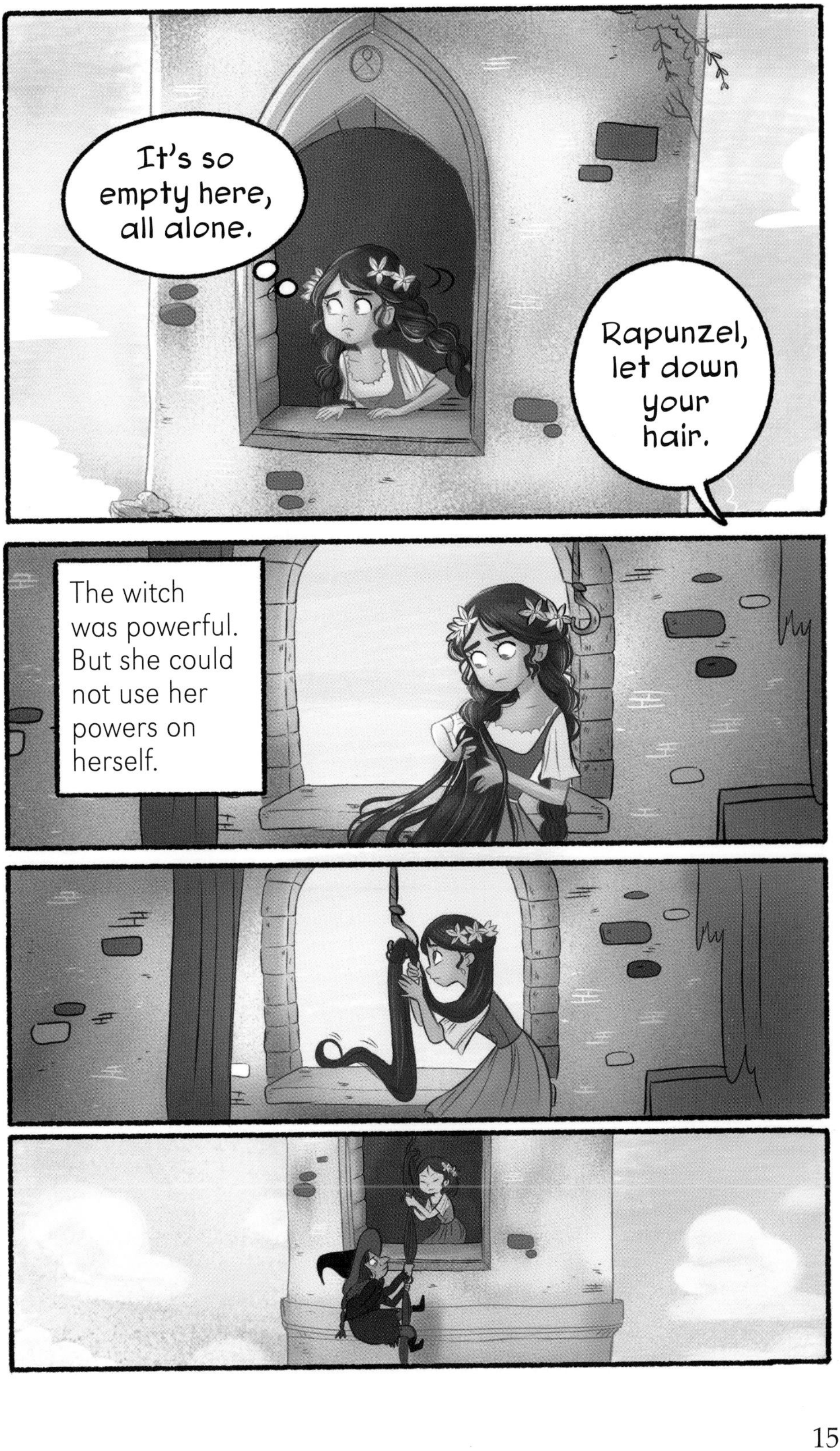
It's so empty here, all alone.
Rapunzel, let down your hair.
The witch was powerful. But she could not use her powers on herself.

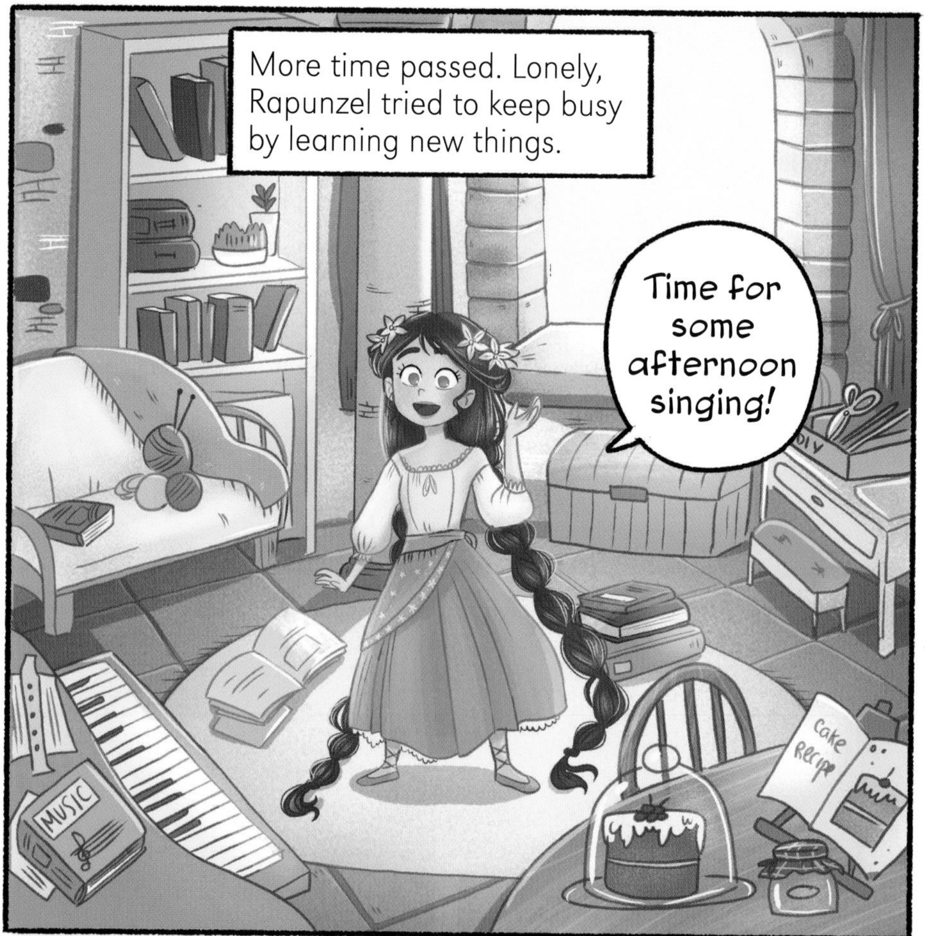
More time passed. Lonely, Rapunzel tried to keep busy by learning new things.
Time for some afternoon singing!
MUSIC
Cake Recipe
DIY

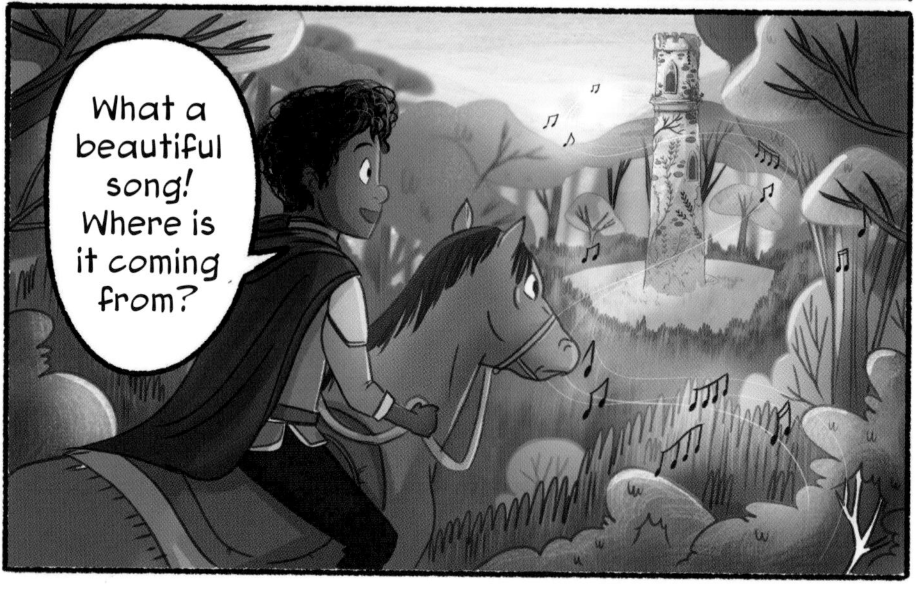
What a beautiful song! Where is it coming from?

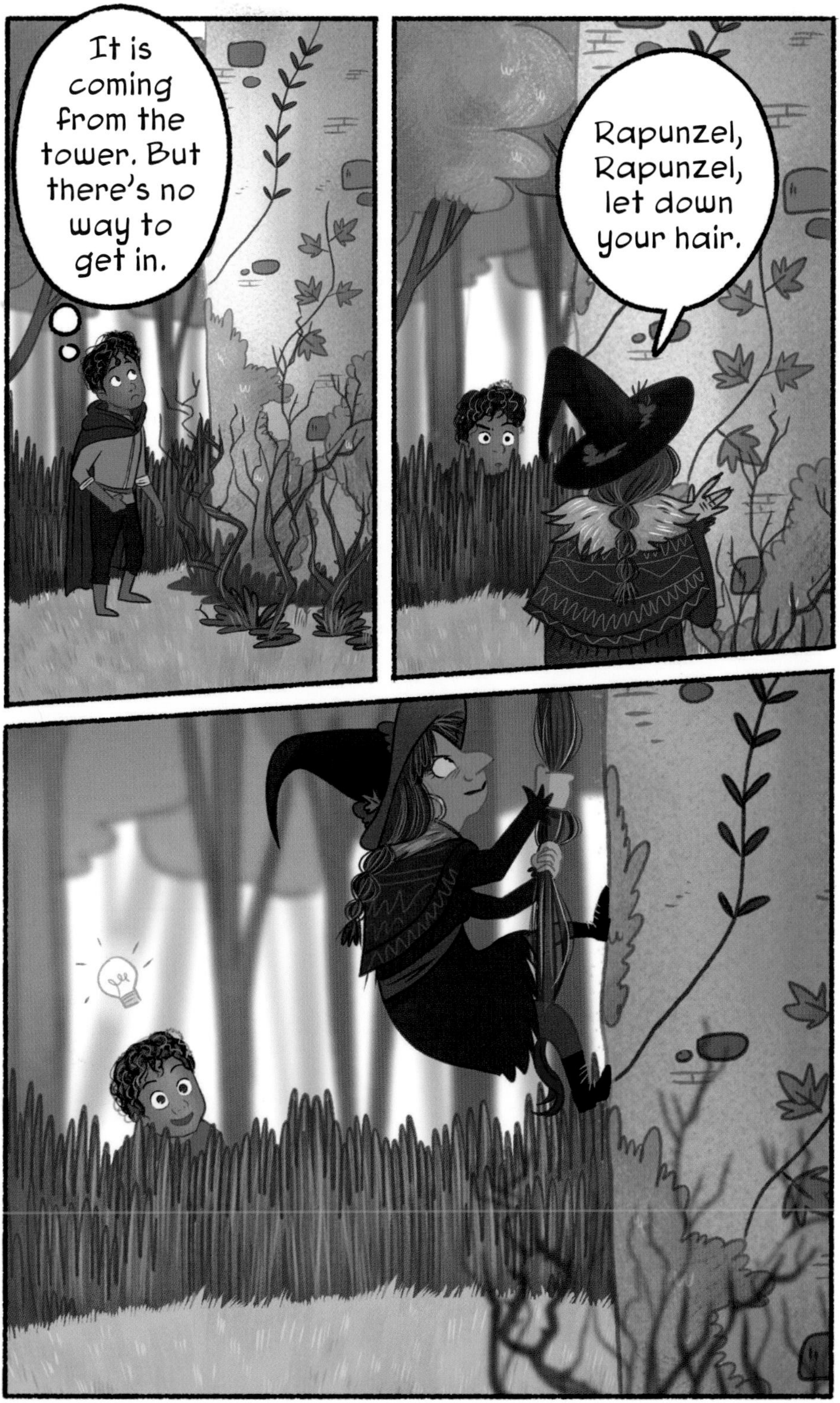
It is coming from the tower. But there's no way to get in.
Rapunzel, Rapunzel, let down your hair.

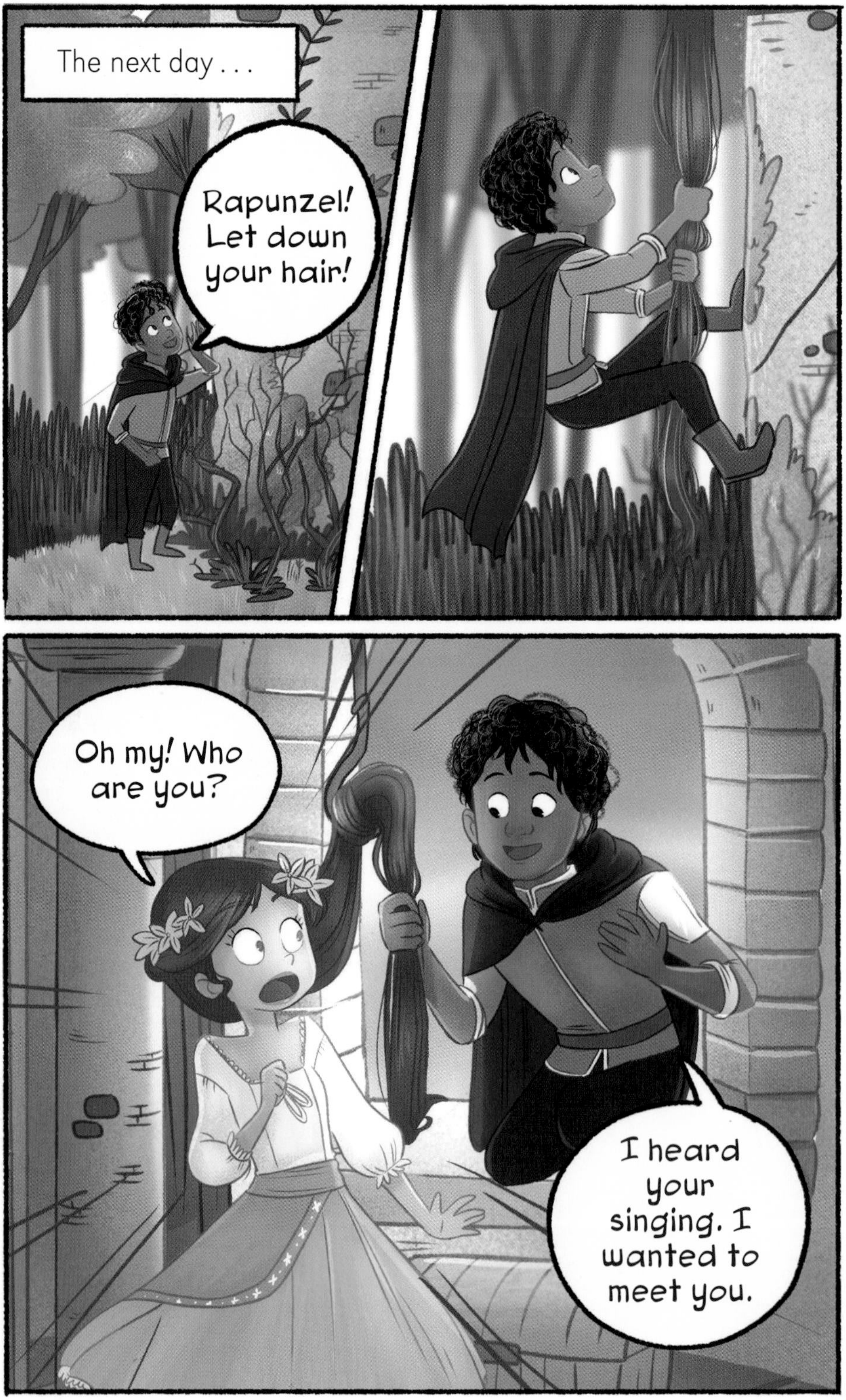
The next day . . .
Rapunzel! Let down your hair!
Oh my! Who are you?
I heard your singing. I wanted to meet you.

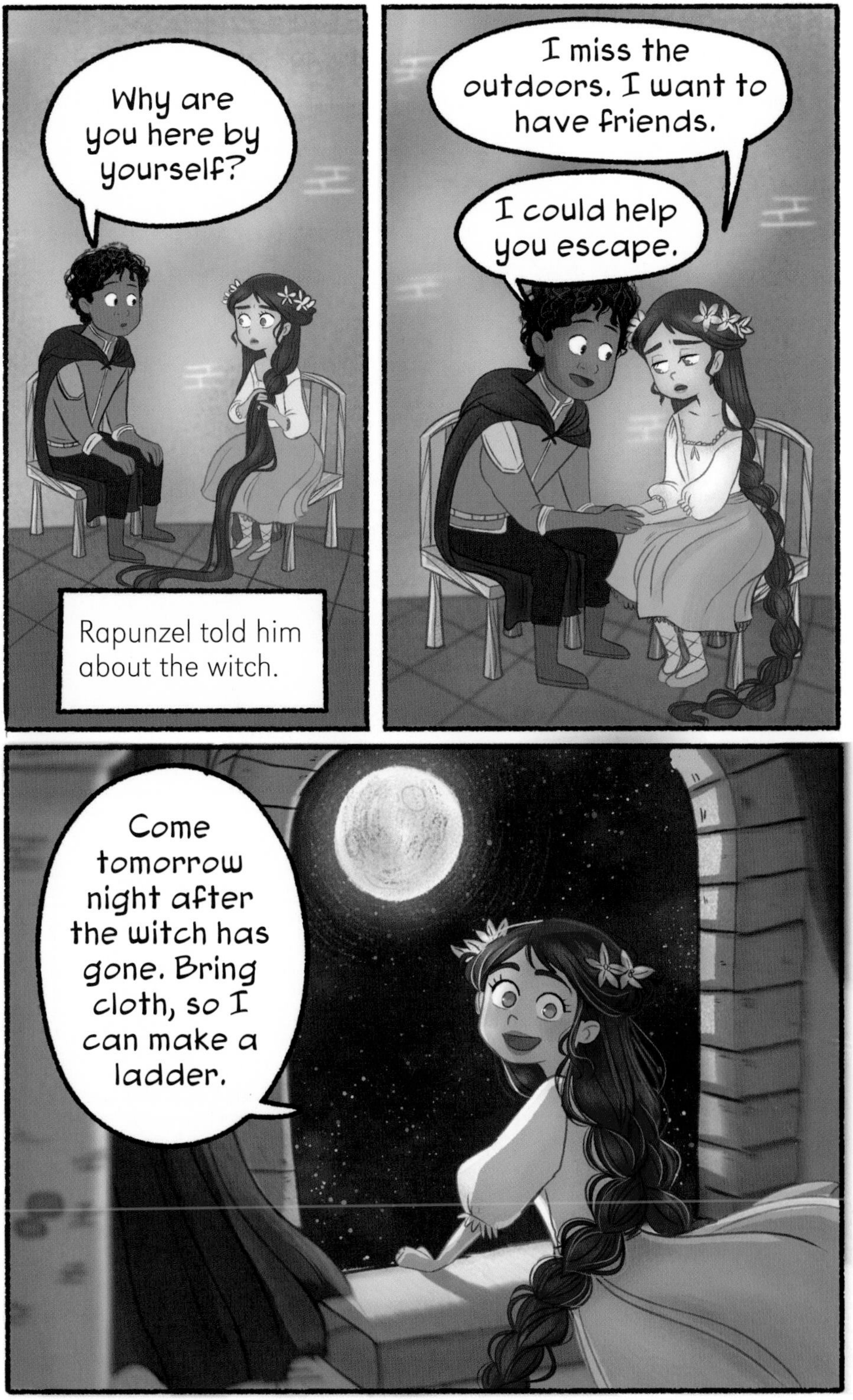
Why are you here by yourself?
Rapunzel told him about the witch.
I miss the outdoors. I want to have friends.
I could help you escape.
Come tomorrow night after the witch has gone. Bring cloth, so I can make a ladder.

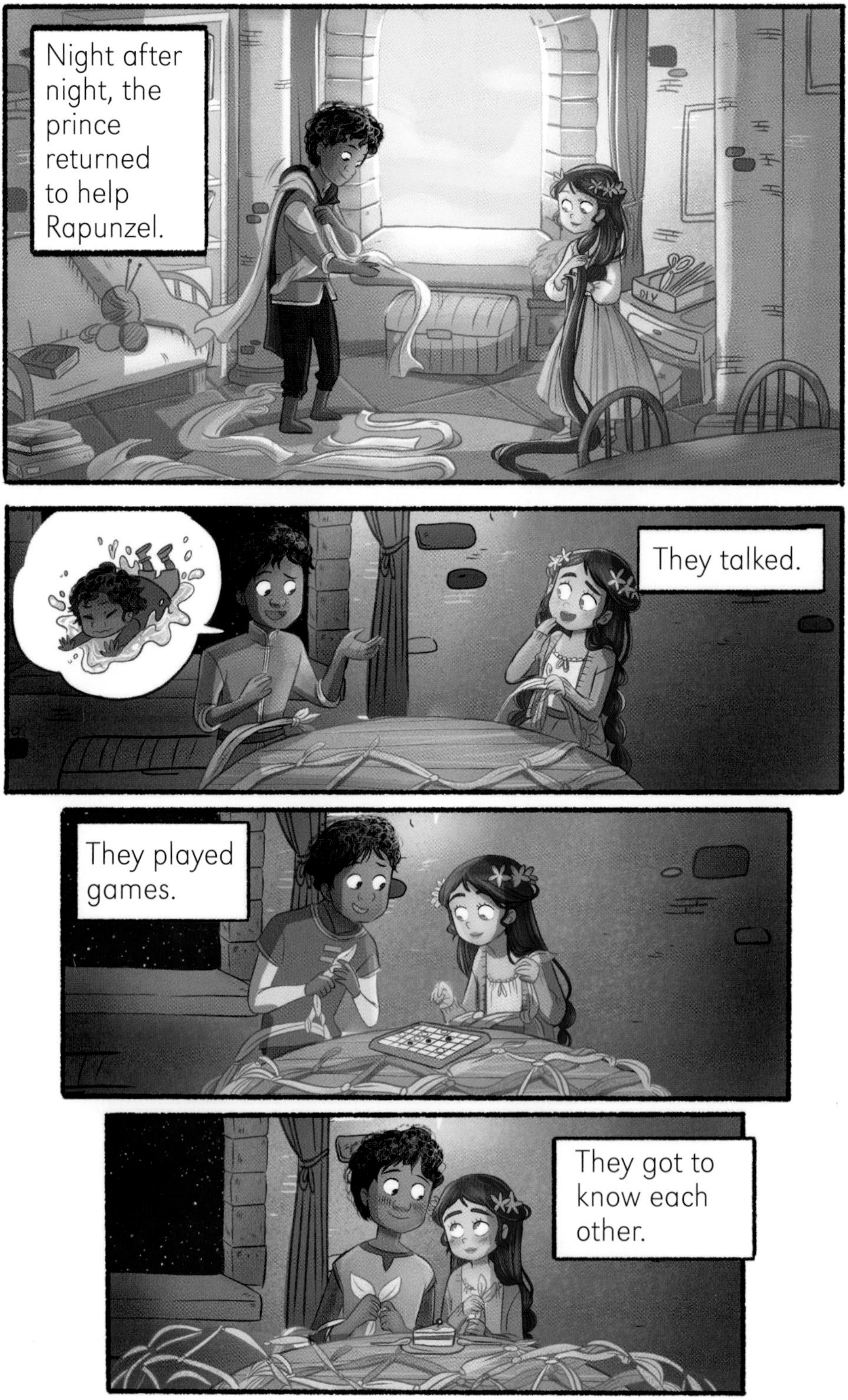
Night after night, the prince returned to help Rapunzel.
They talked.
They played games.
They got to know each other.

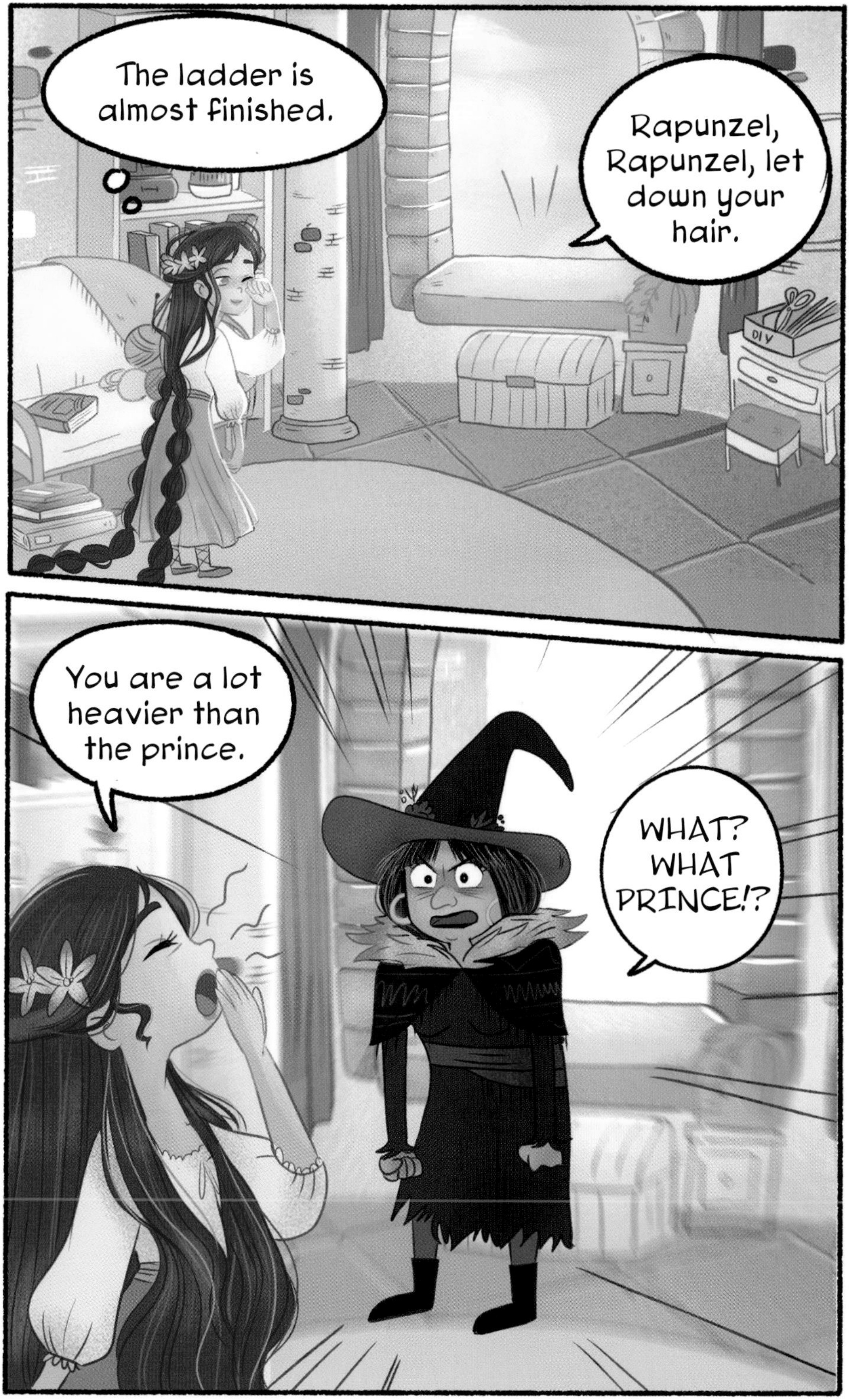
The ladder is almost finished.
Rapunzel, Rapunzel, let down your hair.
DIY
You are a lot heavier than the prince.
WHAT? WHAT PRINCE!?

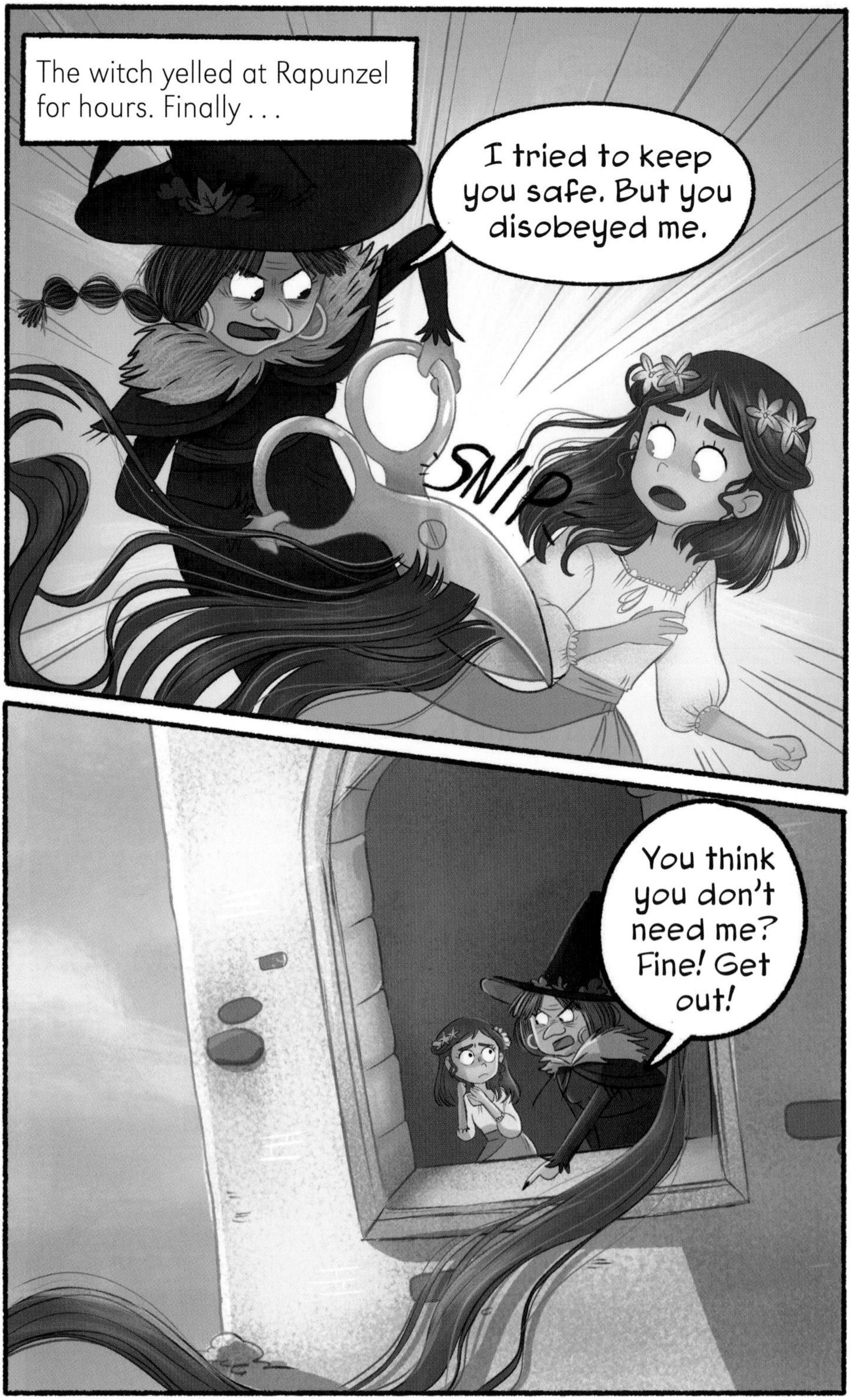
The witch yelled at Rapunzel for hours. Finally . . .
I tried to keep you safe. But you disobeyed me.
SNIP
You think you don't need me? Fine! Get out!

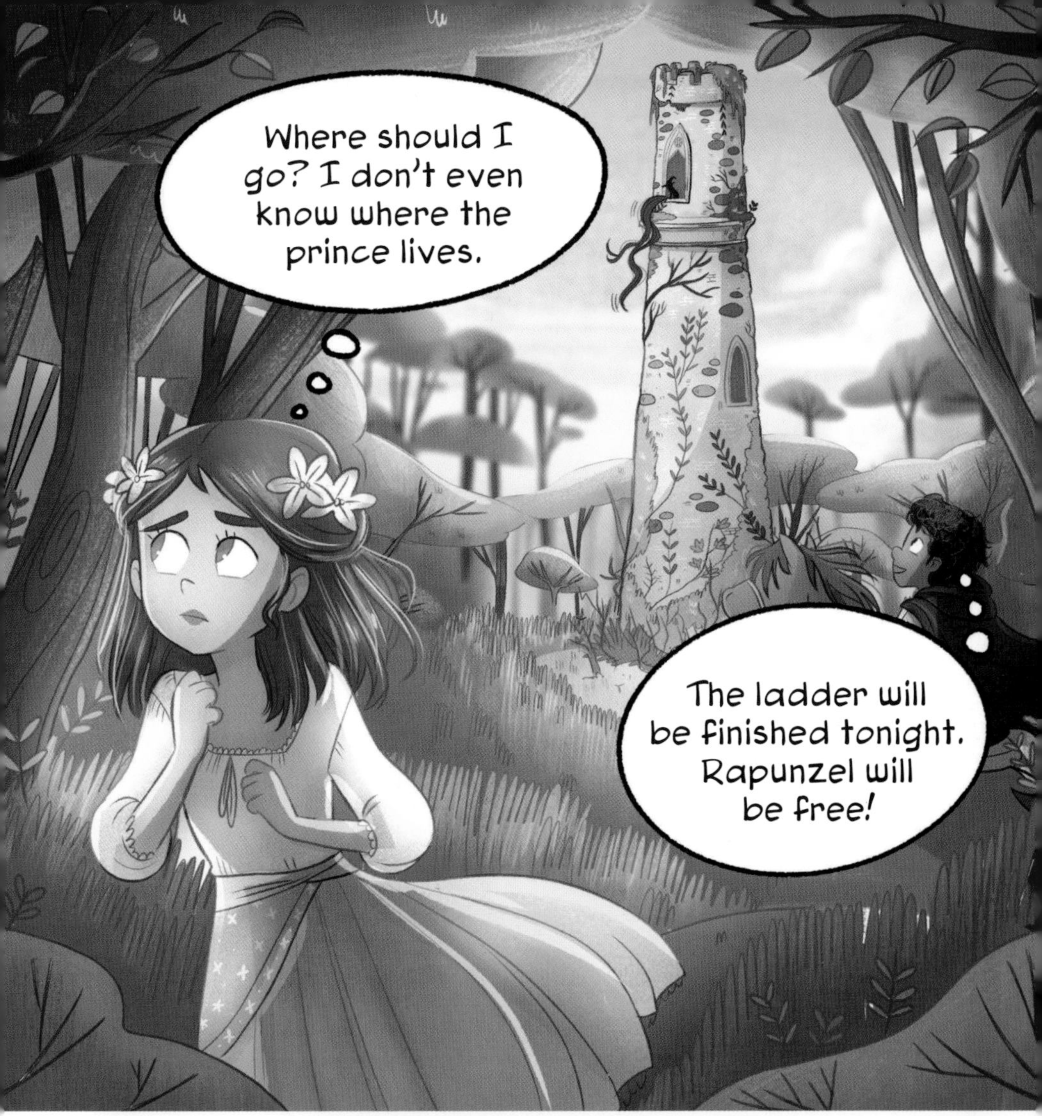
Where should I go? I don't even know where the prince lives.
The ladder will be finished tonight. Rapunzel will be free!

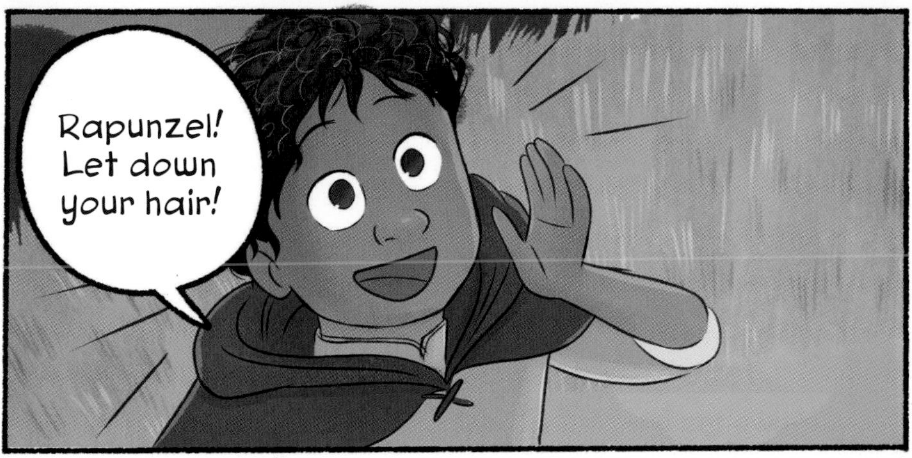
Rapunzel! Let down your hair!

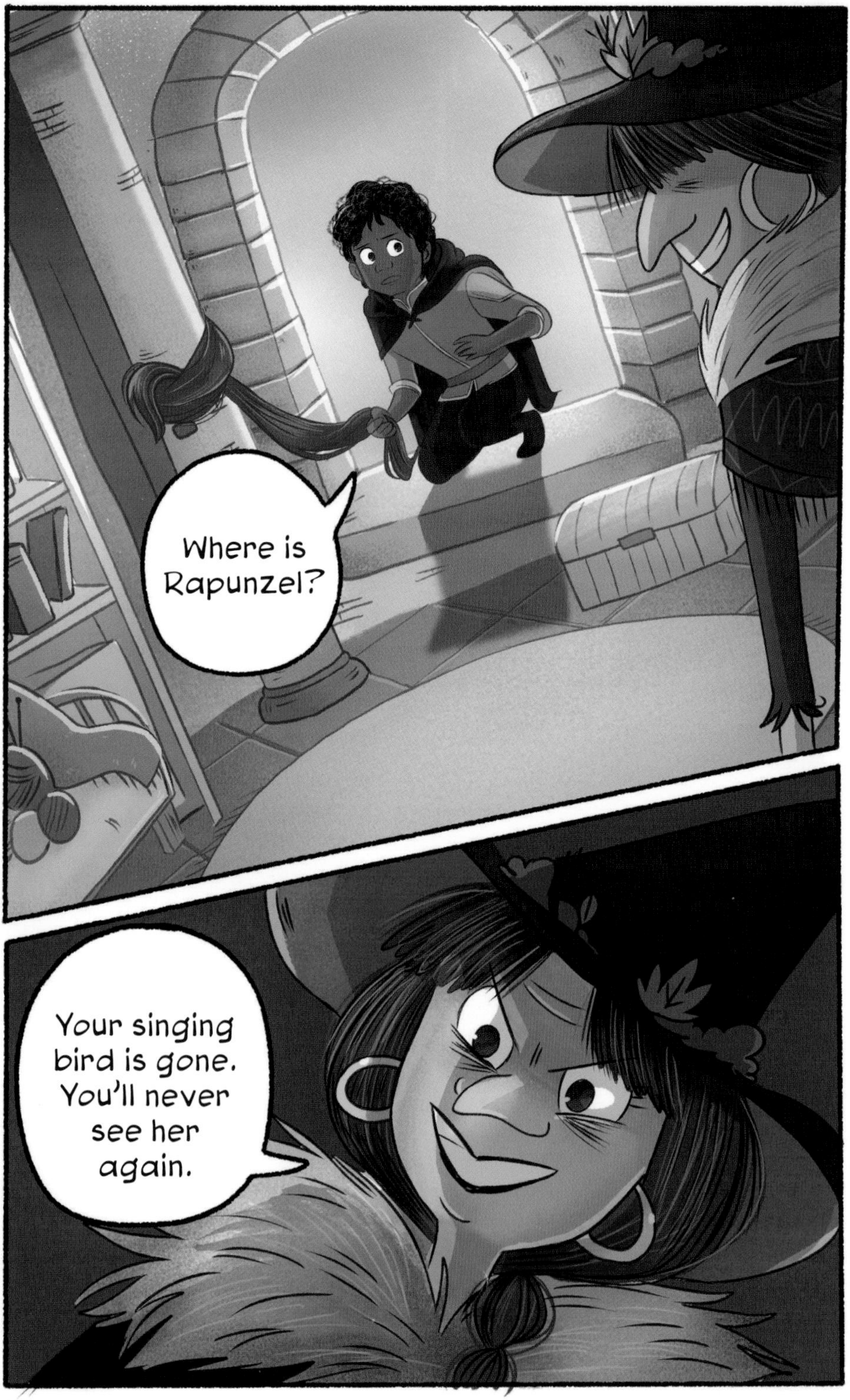
Where is Rapunzel?
Your singing bird is gone. You'll never see her again.

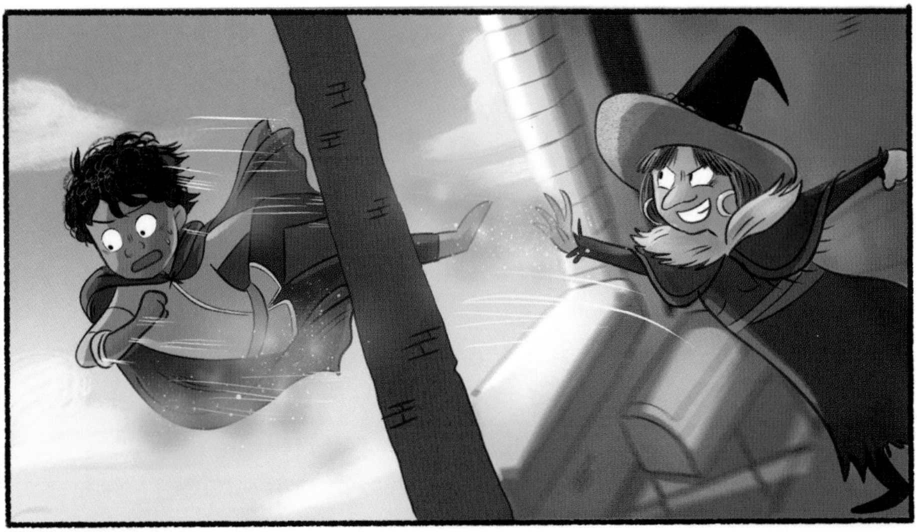

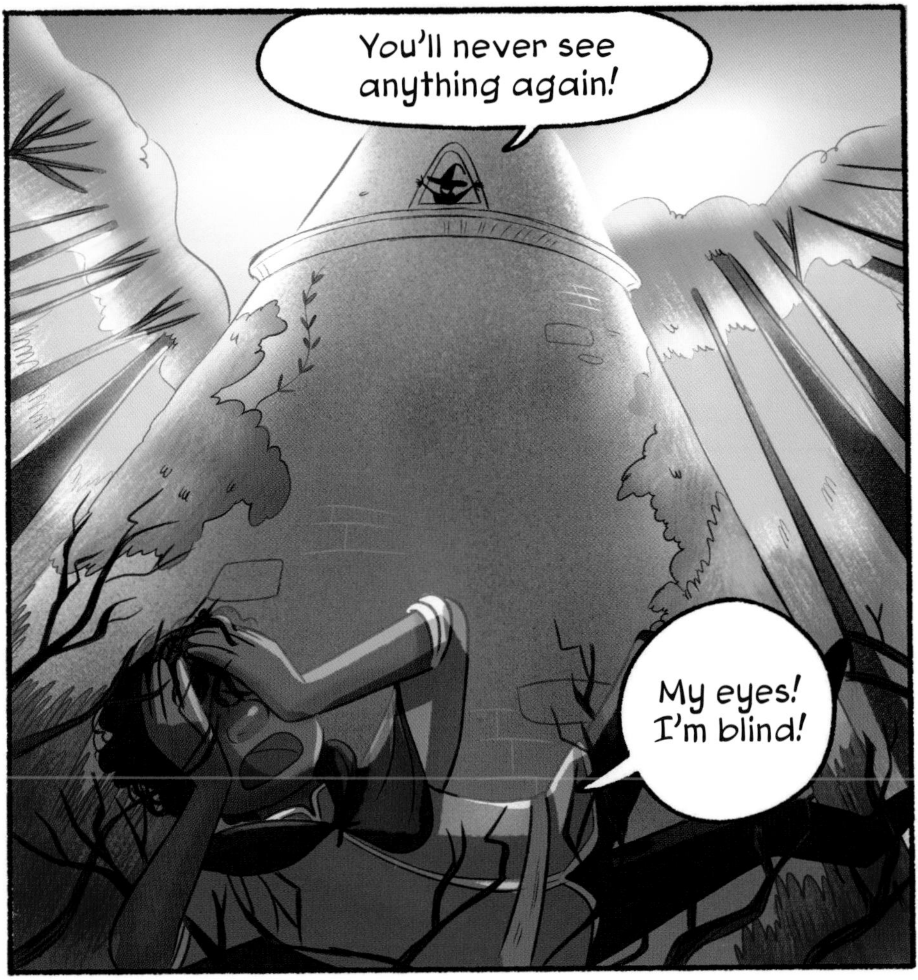
You'll never see anything again!
My eyes! I'm blind!

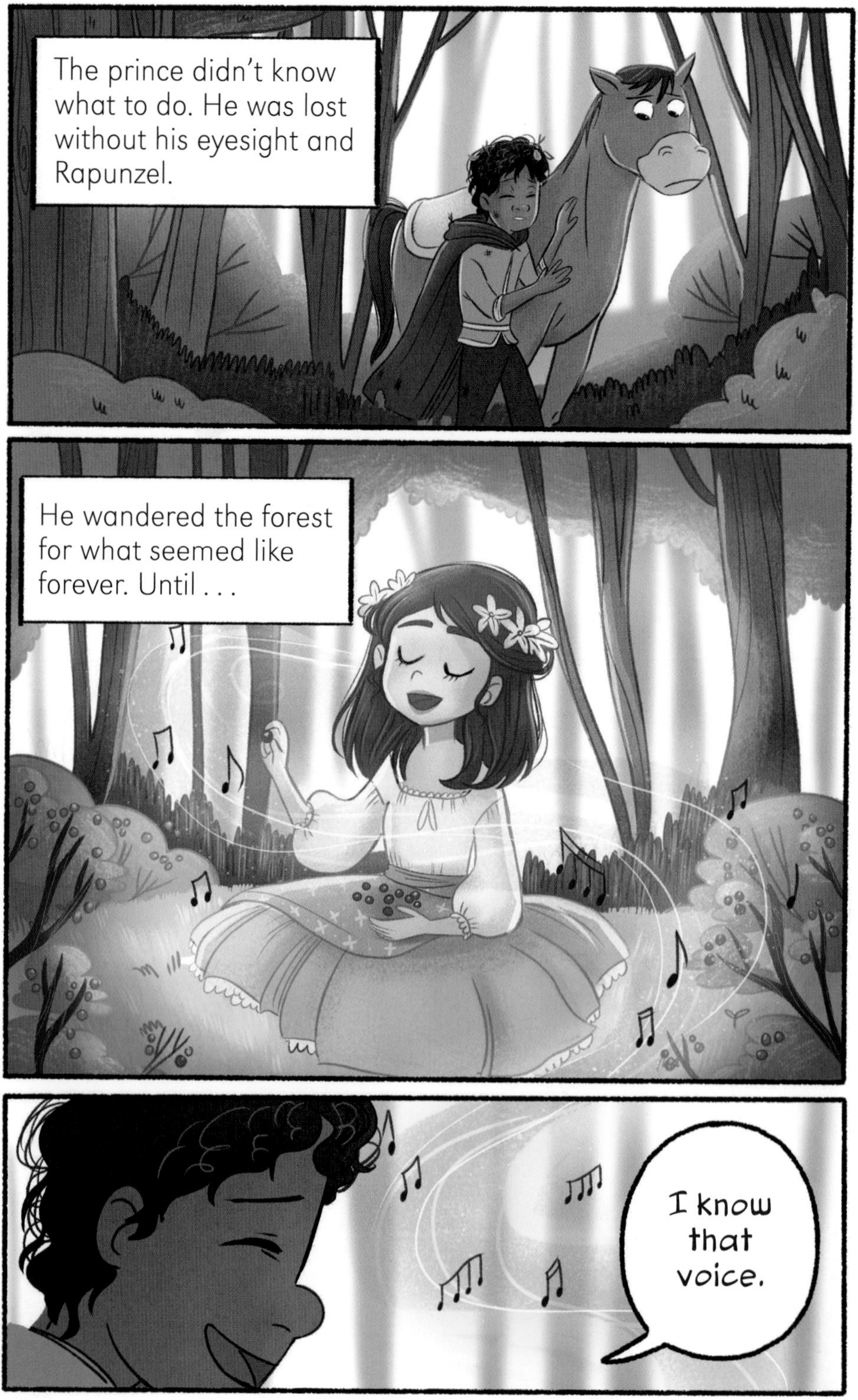
The prince didn't know what to do. He was lost without his eyesight and Rapunzel.
He wandered the forest for what seemed like forever. Until . . .
I know that voice.

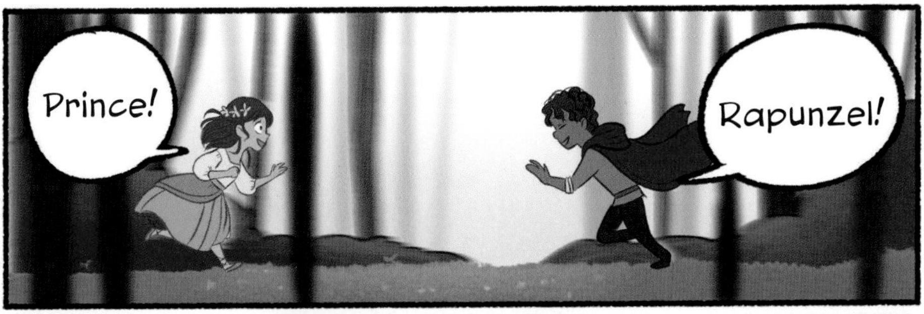
Prince!
Rapunzel!

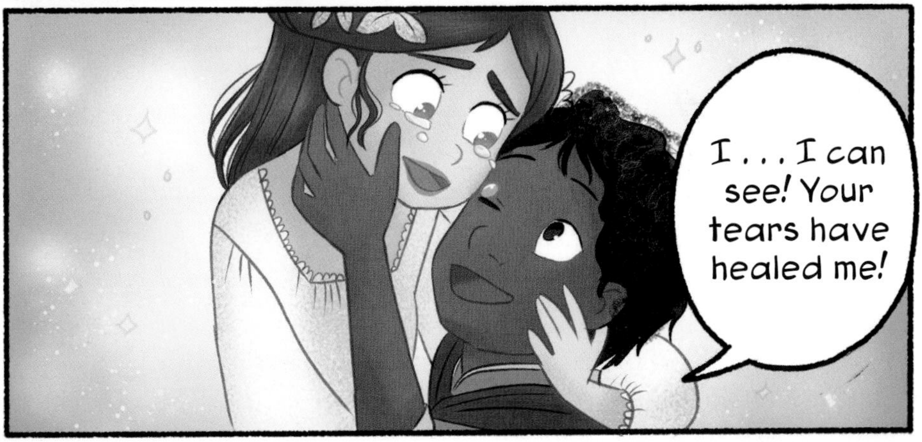
I . . . I can see! Your tears have healed me!

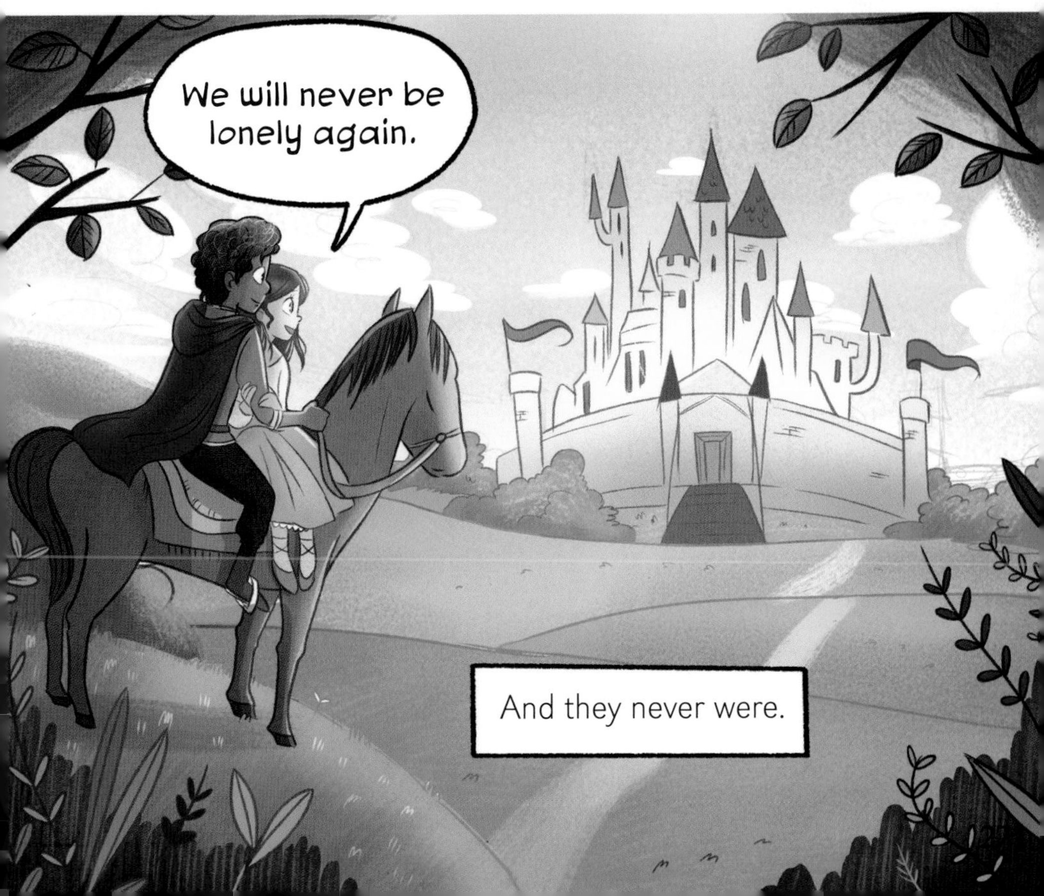
We will never be lonely again.
And they never were.

WRITING PROMPTS

1. What would you do to keep busy if you were locked in a tower? Make a list. Think of things you could do indoors and by yourself.

2. Write a story from the witch's point of view. How would you feel if one of your neighbors took something that belonged to you?

3. Pretend you are Rapunzel. Write a letter to a friend describing the people around you. How would you describe the prince? The witch? Tell your friend about life in the tower.

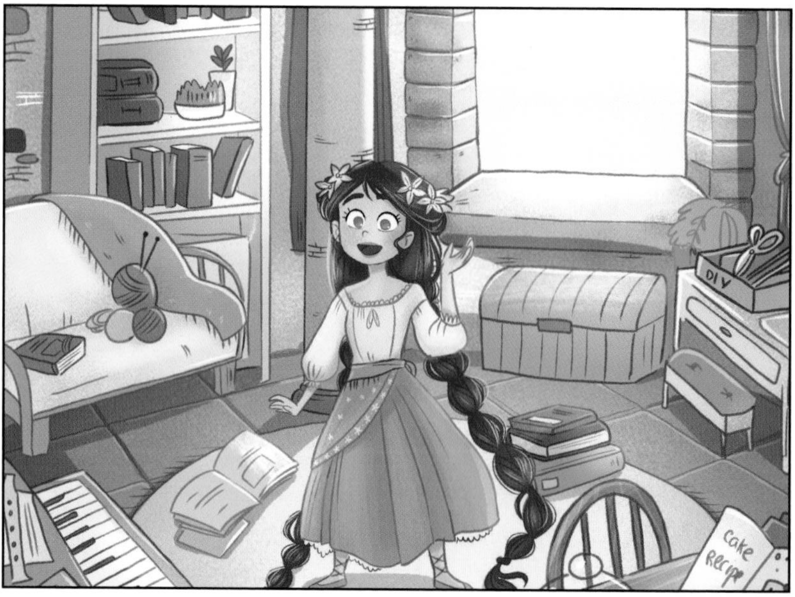
Cake

DISCUSSION QUESTIONS

1. Talk to an adult about promises. Are there promises that are too big to keep? Is it okay to break some promises? How do you feel when you keep a promise?

2. Why do you think the prince wanted to help Rapunzel?

3. Have you ever been really hungry for something, like Rapunzel's mother was? Draw a picture of it. How did you feel when you finally got it?

LET DOWN YOUR HAIR

Rapunzel's hair was strong enough to hold a person. Could floss, embroidery thread, or yarn do the same thing? Find out which material is the strongest with this simple test.

WHAT YOU NEED:

- 1 foot- (0.3-meter)-long pieces of floss, embroidery thread, and yarn
- three heavy rocks of similar weight

WHAT YOU DO:

Step 1: Guess which material you think will be the strongest. Why? Write down your choice.

Step 2: Tie the floss around a rock. Make sure the rock is secure.

Step 3: Tie the thread around the second rock.

Step 4: Tie the yarn around the third rock.

Step 5: Measure the length of the floss, thread, and yarn. Write down your measurements.

Step 6: Gently pick up the loose end of the floss. Let the rock hang in the air.

Step 7: Repeat step 6 with the thread, and then with the yarn. Did the floss, thread, or yarn break?

Step 8: If none broke, re-measure the lengths of the floss, thread, and yarn. The one that stretched the most is the weakest.

READ ALL THE AMAZING BOOKS IN THIS SERIES

CINDERELLA
DISCOVER DG GRAPHICS
WRITTEN BY JENNIFER FANDEL ILLUSTRATED BY MICHELLE SIMPSON

BEAUTY and the BEAST
DISCOVER DG GRAPHICS
WRITTEN BY JESSICA GUNDERSON ILLUSTRATED BY THAIS DAMIÃO

RAPUNZEL
DISCOVER DG GRAPHICS
WRITTEN BY JENNIFER FANDEL ILLUSTRATED BY ANUKI LOPEZ

SLEEPING BEAUTY
DISCOVER DG GRAPHICS
WRITTEN BY JESSICA GUNDERSON ILLUSTRATED BY RUSS COX

HANSEL AND GRETEL
DISCOVER DG GRAPHICS
WRITTEN BY JESSICA GUNDERSON ILLUSTRATED BY ALEX LOPEZ

DISCOVER DG GRAPHICS
RED RIDING HOOD
WRITTEN BY CRISTINA OXTRA ILLUSTRATED BY MIGUEL DÍAZ RIVAS

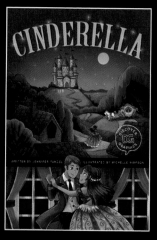

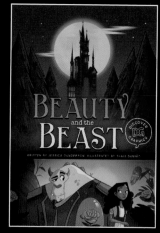

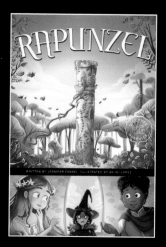

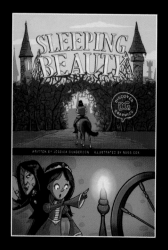

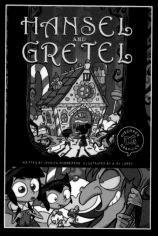

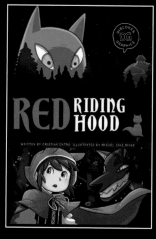